Boot Hill
Book 2
Revenge

Luis Antwoord

Issac O'Connor stands on the porch of the house he once shared with his wife, watching the sun set in the red sky. In the house behind him he can hear his daughter, Abby, milling around in the kitchen, as she fixes their supper. Rubbing his leg, he remembers all too vividly the horrors they both went through not two weeks earlier, but now the Irons' Gang is gone and he hopes they can find peace in Jericho. Abby calls to him from the kitchen that supper is ready, but he stands still, taking in the beautiful sunset and remembering his first gun fight.

~ ~ ~

He was 13 when he was forced into his first gunfight with a man. His father died before he was 12 and his mother was forced to become a prostitute to support him and his younger brother, who was sick. Issac wasn't yet old enough to join a cattle drive, so he did what he could around town to earn money and help out.

Issac emerges from the livery stable after a long day of mucking stalls and forking hay over to the horses. He is tired, but the weight of the dollar in his pocket makes up for it. Walking home, he whistles a tune into the night. Opening the door, he knows right away that something is wrong. He can't see or hear his brother, as he is usually in the setting room playing on the floor or reading by the firelight. Stepping into the house, he hears a small noise from the back of the house coming from the room he shares with his brother.

He runs into the room and finds his mother and brother beaten and broken. His mother is holding his little brother in her arm and crying. He can see right away that his brother is dead. His little skull is caved in on the side and his neck is twisted at an awkward angle. She hears him come into the room and looks up. Issac is taken aback at the sight of his mother's face. She is bleeding from her scalp, one of her eyes is swelled shut and the corner of her mouth is split. Her dress is torn, exposing one of her breasts. Issac averts his eyes and asks her what happened.

She tells him that Sam Bartlett came over for a good time, but he had no money. When his mother told him to leave, he got violent. He struck her in the mouth. Grabbing her by her hair, he started dragging her back to her room. Issac's little brother heard the commotion and charged out of his room, attacking Bartlett. Bartlett kicked him in the head and sent him careening across the room. He then took Issac's mother into the back, raped her and beat her.

As his mother speaks, her face grows more and more pale. When she finishes telling the story, she coughs and blood froths on her lips. She tumbles forward and Issac rushes to catch her. Holding his dying mother in his arms, he strokes her hair and tells her over and over that it's going to be alright. He holds her for a long time before he realizes that she isn't breathing any more. He shakes her and slaps her, but she is gone.

Issac raises his head and screams.

Going into his mother's room, he looks in the bottom drawer of her dresser and finds his dad's pistol. Strapping it around his waist, he walks out into the night, a young boy on his way to hunt and kill a man. He searches most of the night before he finds Bartlett in the Lucky Strike Saloon on the outskirts of town.

Stepping into the saloon, Issac bellows, "BARTLETT!"

Bartlett turns to him. "What the hell is all that noise about son?"

Issac's eyes are dead and cold when he speaks. His voice is barely above a whisper, but everyone in the saloon can hear him.

"You killed my mother and my little brother. Now I'm going to kill you."

Bartlett can see that the boy in front of him isn't joking, and that he's wearing a gun. A gun doesn't care how old the shooter is, it will kill what it's pointed at all the same. He reaches for his gun. People would talk for months about the draw the young man made on Bartlett.

Issac's hand flashes down with ease. He had been practicing with the gun in secret for a couple of years while his mother was away on business. His practice pays off, as the gun comes up fast and centers on Bartlett's stomach. Bartlett takes a step back, his gun still holstered, and clutches his stomach. Raising his hand, he looks at the blood in confusion.

"You shot me you little..."

Bartlett stumbles over backward and hits the floor. Issac calmly walks up to him and levels the gun at his head. The man looks up into the eyes of a boy and sees nothing but death. Issac thumbs the hammer on the revolver and shoots Bartlett through the left eye. Holstering the gun, he looks around the room and speaks.

"This man raped and killed my mother. When my little brother tried to stop him, he kicked him so hard in the head that he crushed his skull. He had it coming."

Someone in the back of the saloon speaks, "We don't doubt your word son, but you best be getting along before the Marshal finds you. You'll hang for killing a man whether he killed your ma and little brother or not."

So Issac ran. He saddled his mother's horse and rode out of town, and joined a cattle outfit a couple miles outside of town.

~~~

The door opens behind him and interrupts his memory.

"Daddy?" Abby asks, her hand touching his shoulder. "Is everything alright?"

Issac turns to face his daughter and is surprised at how beautiful she looks in the light of the setting sun. *This is no place for a girl, no, a woman. She should be in Kansas City or San Francisco wearing the finest dresses and going to parties with her friends, not hold up in some backwater town with no more than 40 people and most of the men too young or too old to be of any interest to her*. He gives her a tired smile.

"Everything's just fine honey."

"Supper is ready."

"Good." He opens the door and motions for her to go in. "I'm starving."

After supper, Issac sits in his chair by the fire smoking a cigarette, as Abby mends one of her dresses. She looks up from her mending and watches her dad, as he inhales deeply from his cigarette. She wants to ask him what exactly happened two weeks ago, but she's afraid he won't want to talk about it. He notices her looking at him and gives her a smile.

"Is something wrong, honey?"

"Nothing Daddy. I was just thinking about tomorrow."

Issac smiles again and lets his thoughts drift to tomorrow, the day he returns to being Sheriff of Jericho. He didn't want the job initially, but he soon realized that he had no money to speak of, and he sure as hell wasn't going to borrow money from his daughter. So tomorrow he would once again assume the mantle of law enforcement of this small town.

As he watched Abby mend her dress, Issac found himself thinking about the remaining members of Irons' Gang that went in search of the mine. He is sure that Red will have heard about the death of his brother by now and will probably come looking for him, but he hopes the others will go their separate ways.

As if she can read his mind, Abby looks up from her sewing and speaks.

"Daddy? What if Red comes back looking for you?"

"Then I'll arrest him for kidnaping and attempted murder, but I don't think he'll be coming back anytime soon, honey."

"I know you're lying, Daddy." Abby fixes him with her mother's stare. "You didn't have to accept the position of Sheriff you know. We could move somewhere else and start a new life. I have a little money from my marriage with Doug that could buy us a small ranch and a few cattle and horses."

"There is no way that I'm letting a daughter of mine support me. I'm not so old that I can't work for myself, and that's the end of it." He stands and flips the butt of his cigarette into the fire. "Don't think any more on the subject, honey. I'm going to bed for the night."

Issac leans down and kisses his daughter on the forehead, just like he used to when she was a little girl. "Goodnight."

"Goodnight, Daddy."

He lies on the bed across from Abby in the sitting room after pulling his boots off. He still isn't able to sleep in the same room he and his wife shared, so he lets Abby sleep in their old room. He drifts off to sleep thinking about tomorrow and the days to come, wondering if his is, in fact, too old to be a Sheriff. His dreams are the same as they have been every night for the last two weeks. In them, Abby gets taken over and over again, but he isn't able to rescue her. He gets shot down in the street, or beat to death by Jorge, or trampled by a charging horse. Tonight is one of the truly horrible ones though. In this dream, he sees Abby get hung from the cottonwoods beside the bridge in town. He is tied to the bridge and forced to watch as his daughter swings at the end of a rope, her eyes bulging as she gasps for air. Issac sits bolt upright, sweat covering his entire body, his breaths coming in raged gasps.

He looks around the room to see if Abby is still beside the fire, but she isn't. It takes him some time to get himself calm. When he feels his heart rate slow, he lays back on his bed with his hands behind his head, but sleep is a long time coming. He drifts off just as the eastern sky is beginning to brighten. Issac is asleep for only minutes before a rooster right outside his window crows to let everyone know that the sun is coming up. He contemplates shooting the rooster, as he pads over to the fireplace to stir the coals, but he figures that the neighbors won't take too kindly to him shooting their rooster, Sheriff or no Sheriff. Chuckling to himself, he adds a few sticks of wood to the fire and gets water boiling for coffee. While the water boils, he puts on a pair of pants and a clean black shirt. Sitting on the edge of the bed, he turns his boot over and thumps them to rid them of spiders or scorpions that may have taken refuge inside during the night. Pulling on his boots, he shakes his head. *I guess some habits die hard.*

An hour later, Issac stands on the porch of the jail with a small crowd gathered in front of him. Beside him stands Sam Tiller, the founder and unofficial mayor of Jericho.

"Seems like we've been here before ain't we, Issac." Sam chuckles and spits a stream of tobacco into the dusty street. "Well, I ain't much on ceremony, so here it is."

He hands Issac a sliver star. Issac looks out over the crowd and catching Abby's eye, gives her a big smile.

"Thanks Sam." He pins the star on and looks out over the crowd. "Thanks for coming out today folks. Sorry we took so much of your time. I guess I've got work to do, so I reckon I'll talk to you all later."

A choir of 'welcome backs' and 'glad to have

you' comes from the crowd, along with some clapping and a few yells.

"Glad to have you back Sheriff."

"Good luck."

"Stop by any time, Sheriff. Drinks are on the house."

The crowd slowly disperses and mills back to their homes or businesses. They walk in groups of twos and threes, discussing events and people. Abby and a few men climb the steps to the jailhouse porch. Sam gives him a handshake and saunters off the porch toward his rocking chair in front of his house, where he spends most of his days now. Henry shakes his hand and wishes him well before walking back to his general store. Of the five people standing on the porch talking to him, Issac knows all but one. A slender man in the back of the group with his hat pulled down low so that it shades his face.

The slender man steps forward, shoving aside Mort, the bartender, and Gentry, the livery owner. They stumble back with a cry of surprise.

Abby is standing with her arm locked in her dad's when the man makes his move. The man's hat is knocked off by one of Mort's hands, as he stumbles backward, flailing his arms for balance.

Issac recognizes the man at once. Not a man at all, but Jessie from the Irons' Gang.

"You killed my Randy and now I'm going to kill you."

Sunlight flashes off the blade of her Bowie, as she thrusts it at Issac's stomach. He prepares for the impact of the blade, but someone shoves him roughly from the side. His foot hooks on a loose board causing him to fall headlong off the porch. Lights flash in his skull, as his head hits a rock jutting out of the street. A scream sounds behind him. He struggles and gains his feet. Blood runs down the side of his face, as he shakes his head, trying to clear his vision. What he sees makes his knees weak.

Abby lies on the porch, her delicate hands clutching the handle of Jessie's Bowie knife. Mort and Gentry are bent over her. Mort yells something about Doc Blaine and Gentry leaps off the porch running full out. Jessie is nowhere to be seen. Issac starts for the porch on shaking knees, but movement at the corner of his vision draws his eye and makes him turn.

Jessie is riding at him in a dead run with a shotgun in her hands. Issac's left hand drops and grasps the handle of his gun, the only one he is wearing today. His gun comes up fast, but Jessie is already upon him. He stares right into the barrels of her shotgun. His gun bucks twice in his hand and he sees fire belch from the shotgun. Something hits him hard in the right arm, spinning him around. He watches Jessie's horse run out of town, but Jessie isn't in the saddle. He tries to turn and see where she is and drops his gun in the dirt. He stares at it with a look of bewilderment on his face. A cry comes again from the porch and he remembers his daughter.

Swaying on his feet like a drunk, he makes the steps, but when he tries to step up, he loses his balance and falls face first on the porch. Pain shoots up his right side, but he ignores it. His only thoughts are for Abby.

He pulls himself up to her with his left arm.

"Honey."

She turns her head to him, her face pale and drawn. "Daddy, your arm. You're hurt."

"I'm fine honey. You're gonna be fine too. Gentry's gone to get Doc Blaine and he's gonna fix you up good."

Abby smiles and gives him one of her mother's looks. "You always were a bad liar, Daddy. I'm not going to make it and you know it."

"Honey...Abby, you can't leave me. You're all I have left." Issac reaches out a gnarled, shaking hand and strokes the side of her face. "You can't leave me."

"You'll be just fine, Daddy. You're strong and people are counting on you."

"Abby please..."

Her eyes take on a distant look. "Daddy, do you see Momma?"

"I sure do, honey."

"Doesn't she look beautiful in that dress?"

"Yes she does, Abby."

Abby draws in a ragged breath and looks at her dad, her eyes clearing for a second.

"I love you, daddy." Her breath leaves and her face goes slack.

"Abby?" Issac gives her shoulder a shake. "Honey? I love you. Please don't go. ABBY?!"

Somewhere far off, Mort touches Issac and speaks. "She's gone Issac. She's gone."

"NO! SHE CAN'T BE!" Issac tears away from the man's hold and pulls his daughter into his lap. Stroking her hair and rocking, he whispers to her over and over.

"Come back honey...don't leave me here...please don't leave me."

He holds her until the world around him starts to fade, the edges taking on a gray tint. In the back of his mind, he hears boots thumping on the ground. *They can help Abby.* Then blackness takes him.

~ ~ ~

Red sits by the campfire stirring the coals with a long stick, as Big Bull walks up to the fire. Red is drawn and haggard, his cheeks sunken in from lack of eating. Dark circles rim his eyes from lack of sleep and water. The rest of the gang doesn't dare talk to him for fear of catching him in a bad mood and getting killed. He has already killed one of them over a drink of water.

The man had asked Red if he would throw him his canteen since he was standing by it. Red told him to go to hell, but the man thought he was kidding and called Red a lazy son of a gun. The gaunt gunman turned to the man and quietly told him to take it back. The man laughed and told him to take it easy. Red's hands were a blur of motion as he drew both guns and shot the man twice through the throat.

Big Bull sits down on a log across the fire from Red and waits for the gunman to address him. Red stares into the coals for a full minute before looking up at Bull.

"What's the news from town, Bull?"

"Jessie killed O'Connor's daughter, but he killed Jessie."

"What!?"

Bull flinches at the incredulous tone of the gaunt gunman. "She tried to ride O'Connor down and shoot him with a shotgun, but he got the draw on her and shot her out of the saddle. Shot her in the head too; at a full gallop. Hell of a shot."

"He got lucky." Red looks up at Big Bull, his eyes dancing with fire. "Did she at least hit the son of a bitch?"

"They said that she hit him with both barrels in the right arm. The Doc was trying to save him, but they weren't sure if he could or not. James said he overheard the Doc say that even if he saved the old man's life, he would have to take the arm."

"Good. Maybe that old fool will think twice about messing with us when we ride into town and take it over again."

"Why, Red?" Big Bull summons all of his courage to ask the question. "Why don't we just keep looking for the mine and say to hell with the old man and Jericho?"

"That son of a bitch killed my brother." Red jumps to his feet and stares across the fire at Big Bull, his eyes glaring. "I am to see him dead and the town burnt down around his ears. Send word for the others to get back here as quick as they can."

"It'll take 'em at least a couple of weeks to get back from El Paso, Red."

"Fine. Just send for 'em. Let the old bastard stew over the death of his daughter for a while before I put a bullet in his gullet."

~~~

In the blackness, Issac feels pain in his right arm, but it is far off and distant. He feels like he is floating for a while, but then feels nothing. Voices flow in and out of his ear, but the actual words elude his pain-addled mind. Once he hears himself asking for his daughter, but blackness takes him again.

Issac wakes in a strange room. He looks around the room and sees the white walls and ceiling, and the curtains with flowers on them. *This isn't my house.* His head is aching, so he reaches his right hand up to rub his temples, but the arm won't respond. He tries to lift his head up and look at his arm, but when he lifts his head from the pillow, the whole room spins dizzily. His mouth is dry and he feels like he has a fever. He touches his tongue to his dry lips, but it's just as dry. When he attempts to speak, only a dry croak comes from his throat. Someone comes through the door. He can hear their footsteps.

Doc Blaine steps up to the edge of the bed, his face looming over Issac's. Issac tries to ask about Abby, but he can only croak. Doc Blaine disappears for a moment. He reappears with a glass of water. Tipping it to Issac's mouth, he lets a trickle run out.

"Easy does it, Issac. You don't want to choke.

You'll bust your stitches open and I don't really feel like sewing you back up this morning."

Issac takes a couple small sips of the water before he speaks.

"Where is Abby, Doc?"

Doc Blaine's face takes on a sad look, as he stares down at the old man on the bed.

"Don't worry about that right now, Issac. You just worry about getting better first."

"Dammit Doc. Where is my daughter?"

"She's dead, Issac." Doc Blaine lets out a sigh. "Jessie stabbed her and shot you. Don't you remember?"

Issac tries again to reach his right hand up, this time to grab the Doc, but again his arm refuses to work. "What the hell is wrong with my arm?"

"It isn't there anymore, Issac. I had to amputate it."

"What?"

"Your right arm is gone."

Issac stares up at the ceiling for a moment, as he tries to cope with the news, but his fever=addled mind doesn't seem to comprehend any of it. He looks back at the Doc.

"Where is Abby?"

"She died, Issac. We buried her over at Boot Hill a day ago." Doc Blaine pats him on the shoulder and turns to leave. "Get some rest, Issac. You need it."

"What happened to Jessie?"

"You killed her. Best damned shooting I ever saw."

Issac tries to say something else, but he can already feel himself going back to sleep; the medicine Doc Blaine put in his drink is doing its job. Somewhere in the back of his mind he goes over the bad news with his Sheriff's instincts. *Your daughter's dead, you're a crippl,e and the Irons Gang is probably still out there somewhere led by Red or Big Bull. Are you gonna lay here like an invalid or are you gonna get yourself up and do something about it?*

"Lay here." He answers himself.

When he comes to again, Sharon and Henry are standing beside his bed, looking down at him and speaking softly. He is so drained of energy that he can't even speak to them, and he drifts back into unconsciousness, his mind re-living the death of his daughter over and over again.

He wakes again in the middle of the night, screaming and soaked in sweat. Doc Blaine is beside him mixing some kind of powder into a glass of water. He makes Issac drink it all, and in moments his eyes grow heavy and he fades back into blissful unconsciousness.

The next week passes in much the same way, with him in and out of consciousness, but never really knowing what is going on. Issac asks for his daughter time and again. His fever rises and falls. Doc Blaine worries over him day and night, not sure if the man will pull through. Sometime in the night, Issac's fever finally breaks and Doc Blaine lies down for the first time in a week and a half knowing that his patient is going to pull through, physically at least.

~~~

Issac wakes with the sun shining directly into his eyes and his mouth so dry he feels like he's been eating cotton balls. Beside the bed he sees a night stand with a pitcher filled with water and a glass. He tries to reach for it with his right arm, but nothing happens. Raising his head, he looks down at his side. As he stares at the empty spot beside him on the bed where his arm should be laying and the bandage on his shoulder, he remembers Doc telling him that he had to amputate his arm. *Life's gonna be a hell of a lot harder from now on, but at least I'm not dead.*

That word stops him cold, as he sits up on the edge of the bed.

Suddenly, he remembers that Abby is dead; stabbed by Jessie when he was made Sheriff. He recalls drawing his gun and feeling intense pain, but then there is a blank spot. The next thing he can remember is sitting, with Abby in his lap and her dying words*: "I love you, Daddy."*

The words echo in his head.

Issac drops his head, and for the first time in a long time he cries. The warm tears trace the lines on his weathered face, as he sits on the edge of the bed. His mind turns to the idea of suicide, but he drops it immediately. Never a religious man, he isn't worried about the afterlife implications of suicide. It just isn't in his nature to give up on anything. *Suicide's giving up.* He raises a shaking, calloused hand to wipe away his tears. Staring out the window, he makes a vow. *Ilza. Abigail. I'm going to live my life the best way that I can for you both, and if I find out that any of those left in the Irons' Gang had anything to do with your death, I'll hunt 'em down and kill 'em.*

Pouring himself a glass of water, almost dropping the pitcher from weakness, he drinks it in one great swallow. Feeling a little better, he pours another, but sips this one slowly. As he sits back on the edge of the bed, Doc Blaine enters the room. When he sees that Issac is up, a smile lights up his old, wrinkled face.

"Glad to see you on your feet, Issac."

"Thanks, Doc, but I ain't quite on 'em yet. I almost dropped that pitcher of water trying to pour myself a drink."

"You're dehydrated and malnourished, but that ain't nothing that a good home-cooked meal won't fix. I've got eggs and bacon frying in the kitchen when you're ready."

"I'm not sure I want to eat your food, Doc." Issac gives him a small grin. "In the condition I'm in, it just might kill me."

"You ain't kidding."

Doc Blaine lets out a small laugh, but his face quickly grows solemn. He looks at Issac for a moment before speaking, sadness showing in his eyes.

"How much do you recall from…"

Issac stops the doctor with a raised hand. "I remember enough, and that's all I want to say."

"Alright, Issac. Whenever you're ready, come into the kitchen and we'll have us a bite to eat and a couple cups of coffee."

"Sounds good."

Doc Blaine leaves the room, while Issac tries to go about the process of dressing himself, but he finds that doing so with one arm, even with your dominant one, is not easy. Getting his shirt on isn't too bad, but he can't figure out what to do with the right sleeve, and he hates the way it just dangles down his side. *Maybe I can get Deborah or Sharon to fix it for me 'cause that thing dangling down like that will get caught on something eventually.* He puts on his pants, pulling them up a little at a time. He tries to put on his gun belt, but he can't do the buckle. Embarrassed and frustrated, he lays it back on the bed. His left boot goes on pretty smoothly, but when he has to reach across his body to pull on his right one he hits some snags. Tugging and twisting, he finally gets the boot on, but in his weakened state, he's panting and sweating by the time he does.

Carrying his gun belt into the kitchen, he finds Doc already sitting at the table with two plates full of food and two steaming cups of coffee. He lays his gun belt on the table and sits down, letting out a sigh of relief. Issac eats quickly and gulps the scalding coffee. Black, just the way he likes it. He only eats a couple of eggs and a few slices of bacon before his stomach cramps up. It has shrunk from a lack of food during his recovery. He sits back in his chair and sips the coffee, as Doc Blaine, who has no problem eating his share and what is left of Issac's, finishes his meal.

"This is good coffee, Doc. Strong, just the way I like it."

"My pa used to say that good coffee should be able to float a horseshoe."

"This is good coffee then."

They talk for a while about range conditions and cattle prices, about them fencing off range in Texas and a hundred other things men will talk about given time enough. As they talk, Issac can already feel the food doing its job and making him stronger. After a while, he stands and tells the Doc that he's going home to rest. Placing his gun belt over his left shoulder, he makes his way toward the door.

"Alright, Issac, but I want you back in here tomorrow morning so I can change your bandages and take a look at my stitching to make sure it's still holding."

"Sure thing, Doc. What do I owe you for this?"

Doc Blaine's face takes on an angry look for a moment. "You don't owe me a damned thing, and if you mention paying for anything again I'll take one of your legs too." His face lightens up and he smiles. "We're friends, Issac, and besides, you've saved my hide more than once. I owed you."

"Thanks, Doc." Issac holds out his left hand. The doctor holds out the wrong hand at first out of habit and they both get a good laugh, but they finally shake hands. Issac steps out the door and down the steps. Doc Blaine calls to him as he steps out into the street.

"Don't be doing anything strenuous or you'll

pull your stitches."

He waves a hand in reply, but his mind is already somewhere else; he's trying to figure out if Jessie was still working with Red and the others or if she was acting alone. His sheriff's instincts kick in. *There's no way you can know now that she's dead, but you could talk to Mort. He hears a lot of talk in his bar.* Issac decides to talk to Mort and see if he has heard any talk about Red or Big Bull, but not right now. All he wants to do right now is go home and sleep in his own bed.

A few people speak to him on the street, but he tries to avoid most of them. The ones he can't avoid he speaks only long enough to say hello. When he finally steps inside his house, he breathes a sigh of relief. He is more exhausted from the walk across town than he can believe is possible. He Pulls his boots off and tosses his gun belt on his chair. Without realizing it, he stumbles into his old room, the one he shared with his wife and the one his daughter used until recently. He lies down, and within seconds he is sleeping soundly.

The first thing Issac notes when he awakes the next morning is the pain in his shoulder. It hurt some the day before, but this morning it is throbbing. Sitting up on the edge of the bed, he looks around the room and realizes which room he is in. On the dresser is a picture from his wedding day of his wife in a white dress. Reaching out a hand, he takes the picture and examines it. He rubs a thumb across the glass and speaks, "I'll get whoever is responsible for Abby's death, Ilza. I promise."

Issac makes his way into the sitting room and goes about building a fire. Getting the wood isn't too hard, but lighting a match is a nightmare. In the end, he has to hold the matchbox between his socked feet so he can strike the match. With the fire going, he puts on water to boil for coffee. Instead of boots, he pulls on an old pair of moccasins; they're quiet and a hell of a lot easier to get on than boots. *I reckon this morning will be as good as any to go see Mort and ask about Red and the others.*

Sipping his cup of coffee, he looks at his gun

belt and tries to figure out how he's going to get it strapped around his waist. He can't work the buckle with one hand. He finally decides to just shove the pistol down in the waistband of his jeans and put a handful of shells in his left pocket. *A good thing I've got these Schofields. Any other pistol I wouldn't be able to unload.* Looking around, he realizes that he doesn't have a hat, at least not in his house. *I must have left it at the Doc's. I'll get it when I get my bandages replaced.*

Outside the air is cool, but not cold. It feels great on his lungs after being cooped up in a house for a week and a half. The walk to Doc Blaine's isn't a long one, but due to his weakness, it takes him much longer than it should. Issac is starting to sweat and breathe hard when he steps onto the doctor's porch. Doc answers on the first knock, his shirt untucked and his hair disheveled.

"Issac, how are you this morning?"

"I can't complain."

"Good. Good. Come on in. I've got some

coffee on. I'll change those bandages and take a look at my stitching while it's percolating."

"Sounds good." Issac is eager to be away, but he knows that he owes this man his life. He figures that another 20 minutes isn't going to hurt his investigation.

Inside, the doctor points at the kitchen and tells Issac to have a seat while he fetches his bag from his room. Sitting and waiting for the Doc, Issac looks around for his hat, but can't see it anywhere. The Doc comes from the back room with Issac's hat and a large black bag in his hands.

"Here." He hands the hat over to Issac. "You left this here yesterday."

"Thanks." He lays the hat on the table and pulls his shirt off.

He watches, as Doc Blaine removes the old bandages and checks the stitching on his shoulder. The doctor looks for a while, not speaking, before he retrieves clean bandages from his bag. Carefully, he applies some kind of cream that smells to high heaven and wraps the shoulder in the bandages. When he finishes, he leaves Issac to put his shirt back on while he brings coffee back.

The two men sit and talk for an hour or more. Issac is eager to get away, but he doesn't want the doctor to know what he's planning. Finishing his cigarette, he snubs it out in the turtle shell the Doc gave him for an ashtray.

He stands up. "I think I'll be getting to the house after I stop by Deborah's and see if she can fix me some shirts."

"She's already working on it." Doc Blaine gives him a grin.

"How's that?"

"When she saw that you were going to lose your arm, she went to work a fixing shirts without a right sleeve for you. I'll let you go, Issac." He opens the door and steps back to let Issac go through. "But remember, nothing strenuous."

"Sure thing, Doc."

Issac steps out into the street, the sunlight

warming him in the cool morning air, and finds that all things considered he doesn't feel half bad. He hears the pounding of hooves from behind. Spinning around, he drops his hand to his pistol, thinking that it was Red or one of the others from the gang, but he doesn't recognize either of the riders. They thunder past him and up to the saloon. Shaking his head, he walks across the street to Deborah's and opens the door.

Inside, the store smells beautiful, like a woman, soft and delicate. Issac stands in the doorway for a second, letting his eyes adjust to the light inside the store. A short, squat woman with bright red hair appears from a room behind the counter. When she sees him standing there, her face lights up and she rounds the counter at a fast pace. Without a word, she walks right up to him and wraps him up in a hug.

"How are you doing, Sheriff?"

"I'm okay, Deborah."

"If there is anything that you need, you just ask." She steps back and looks him in the eye. "I mean it, Sheriff."

"Now that you mention it." He gives her a grin and points to his limp sleeve. "There just might be something that you can do for me."

"Of course. Of course." She hurries around the counter. "Wait right there."

Issac stands by the counter and listens to the short woman in the back rummaging around. Something falls and she mutters under her breath, but she returns quickly with a bundle in her arms. Deborah lays it on the counter, talking as she unties the strings.

"I was going to bring this to your house today, but since you're already here, I guess...now come lose you darn thing...I'll let you have 'em now."

She finally gets the parcel open and inside is three shirts: one red, one black, and one brown. She selects the brown one and holds it out to Issac.

"Try it on and see how it fits."

He takes the shirt, as he looks around. "Is there a room I can change in?"

"You can change right here, Sheriff." She gives him a knowing grin. "I've seen men without their shirts on before and haven't fainted. You just go on ahead and change into that shirt."

"It won't look right, Deborah. Me in here with my shirt off and you standing there. What if someone should come in?"

"Then they can get over it or get out. Now try that shirt on."

Issac can feel his cheeks burning, as he slips his old shirt over his head, revealing a well-built upper torso for an older man. Laying his old shirt on the counter, he takes the light brown shirt and pulls it over his head, a feat that isn't as easy as it used to be, but he manages just fine. Pulling the shirt down, he marvels at the fit of it. He expects to see stitching or a patch when he looks at the right shoulder of his shirt, but there isn't any.

"Deborah, you made these?" He asks, feeling a lump in his throat at the kindness of this woman.

"I did, but enough of that, turn around and

let me see how it fits in the back."

He spins around and lets her see the back. She plucks and pulls at his shirt for a moment before deciding that it is 'just passable' and 'will do' in her words. She folds his old shirt and lays it on the others. He asks her how much he owes her, as she re-ties the parcel. She looks up at him with hurt eyes.

"Sheriff, how could you ask a thing like that?" He starts to speak, but she cuts him off. "I did this for you and I don't want a thing for it, and if you say something about paying for them shirts again I'll whip you right out of my store with a broom, arm gone or no arm gone."

Smiling at the kindness and generosity of this small woman, Issac tells her he is going home and thanks her for the shirts. He walks out into the street. He thinks about going home, but he gets a glance at Boot Hill, where his daughter is buried, and changes his mind. Turning left, he walks up the street to the saloon. He is passing the general store when a voice from inside stops him.

"Sheriff!"

He stops and looks. Henry comes rushing around the counter with something in his hand. As he gets closer, Issac can see that it's a gun belt. Henry hurries up to him and holds the gun belt out.

"Here, Sheriff."

"Thanks Henry, but I can't wear that. I can't even get it on by myself."

"Oh, I bet you can. I made this special. Look. I made a little leather hook that holds onto your jeans while you use this small string here to put it around your waist with your other hand. There isn't a buckle; I made it with a peg and loop. You just slip the loop over the peg and the weight of the holster keeps it taught. Try it."

Issac takes the belt and studies it for a moment. Slipping the hook into the front of his jeans, he takes the string in his hand and pulls it over his head. He loops it around like he's swinging a lariat and the belt comes around his waist. Grabbing the other end of the belt, he puts the loop over the peg with a hook on it and lets the belt settle into place. It fits like a dream. Pulling his pistol from his waist, he holsters it. He draws it and holsters it again.

"It's perfect, Henry. You did a hell of a job on this. I can't thank you enough."

"Don't mention it, Sheriff. That string tucks into a small pocket right there in the front of the belt...yeah that one."

"How much-" Issac starts to ask, but Henry stops him mid-sentence.

"Don't even say it, Sheriff, or I'll take it as a personal insult. I did it for you. Now go and do whatever it was you were going to do. I'll talk to you later."

Henry turns without another word and goes back into his store. Issac feels like a brand-new man, as he walks up the street toward the saloon. His sheriff's instincts note the brand on the horses standing out front. *Two Bar B for the Ballard outfit to the west. Three K Bar for the Kent outfit to the northeast. Those two wearing the Clover4 brand are the ones that came riding up the street earlier. Right handy that clover brand. Seems that it could cover up either the Bar B or the K Bar quite easily.*

Issac steps up on the porch and looks through the batwing door of the saloon. Stepping off to the side, he lets his eyes adjust to the darker room. He knows that there really isn't any reason for him to do this, but old habits die hard. As his eyes adjust, he sees the two Bar B riders with drinks in their hands at the bar. Two of the K Bar riders are sitting at a table, eating what looks like stew. The other is standing by the stairs talking to Jenny, one of the women who provide company for men at the Last Chance Saloon. The two unknown riders sit at a table against the wall. One of them is playing solitaire while the other eats. The one playing solitaire is a young man wearing two guns tied down, an unusual thing to see in a cowhand. *By the looks of his outfit outside, he probably isn't a cowhand.* Mort is behind the bar cleaning a mug with a towel.

Issac strolls up and lays his parcel on the bar. Mort turns and looks at him, his face lighting up when he sees who it is.

"Issac! How are you holding up, man?"

"Good enough, Mort. How's about a whiskey?"

"Coming up."

Mort pours him a shot, and Issac tosses it off. Setting his glass down, he motions for Mort to pour another. He drinks this one down and motions for another. This one he lets sit. He speaks to the bartender in a voice just loud enough for him to hear.

"What have you heard about the Irons' Gang?"

"Nothing since you cleared 'em out."

"I mean Red and Big Bull and the others."

"There was a man come in here a couple nights ago, said he heard that Red was running down Santiago way with a big man and a couple others. Said they was rustlin' cattle."

"Santiago. That's a fair piece from here."

"About 40 miles." Mort gives him a flat stare. "Why you asking about Red and the others, Issac? You ain't planning on going after them, are you?"

"No. I was just wondering if they were around. Wanted to know if they would be causing any problems around here, but I guess that isn't my job. Say Mort, who did you get to sheriff when I was shot."

"No one, Issac. Sam said the job was still yours if you wanted it."

"We'll see."

Issac starts to ask Mort something else, but a voice stops him.

"Looks like this town is so desperate for a sheriff that they gotta hire a one-armed man, Lloyd."

"Jesus, Ben."

Issac feels his face turn red, as the two men snicker at the comment. He turns around slowly to face them. He hears Mort tell him to 'let it go', but he realizes where he has seen the brand on their horses before. Randy Houston, Red's brother was riding a horse with that same brand when he rode away from Irons' ranch house. In fact, all the horses in the corral had that same brand. When Issac speaks he does so calmly.

"Where'd you boys say you're from?"

Ben, the one with two tied-down guns, speaks. "I don't see how that's any of your business, cripple."

"No reason to get hostile, son. I was just wondering."

"I ain't your son, old man."

Issac knows that he should back off, but for some reason the devil is driving him and he can't back out. With a growing sense of unease, he hopes the kid draws on him.

"Mighty nice horses you've got out there. Brands are right pretty too. Cover up any brand in these parts without much fuss with that brand if a man took a mind to."

"Just what in the hell are you accusing me of, *cripple!*" Ben jumps up, slamming his chair back against the wall and making the two K Bar riders scramble away from their table and out from between him and Issac.

"You'll wanna set back down before you get hurt, son. I don't have time to baby you."

Issac starts to turn back to Mort, but the young man's voice bellows loudly throughout the bar.

"Cripple or not, I'm gonna kill you, old man."

Issac spins on the balls of his feet and palms his gun before the man can even move. Ben stares across the room into the muzzle of a gun, and for the first time in his life, realizes that he might die. The old man's eyes blaze green, as he stares over the muzzle at Ben. When he speaks, his voice is calm and quiet.

"You made fun, boy. You rode in here on stolen horses. You wanted to make a name for yourself as a gun-hand, but I've seen a hundred like you in a hundred small towns, and all of them ended up the same way, pushing up daisies."

Issac holsters his gun and stares at Ben. "You wanted trouble. Well, now you've got it. If you think you've got the sand, fill you hand, boy."

Ben just stands there with his hands hovering above his gun butts. His face is pale, and he is sweating hard despite the coolness of the saloon. His tongue runs out and wets his lips, but he makes no move for his guns. He wants to make a move for his guns, and Issac can see it in his eyes.

"I said, *FILL YOUR HAND!*" Issac bellows.

Issac let's Ben grab his guns and start bringing them up. His hand is a blur, as he palms his gun and fires. The slug hits the young man in the chest just above the pocket of his shirt, spinning him around. Ben hits the wall and slides down, his guns falling to the floor. Issac turns and faces the other man at the table. Lloyd's hands shoot into the air, as his face grows pale.

"I don't want no trouble, mister."

"What outfit are you riding for?"

"We were riding for Red Houston. He told us

to come into town and tell the Sheriff that he was coming for him, and that this time he was going to finish the job. He spoke to Ben longer than he did me, but I don't know what they talked about."

"Mort, get the undertaker will you?" Issac speaks without turning around. He points his gun toward the door. "Me and you are going down to the jailhouse, and we're gonna have a long talk."

"Alright, mister. Just don't shoot me."

Issac leads the other gunman down to the jailhouse. Motioning for him to get in the cell, he slams the door and locks it. Tossing the keys on the desk, he grabs a chair and sits down in front of the cell. For a moment he doesn't speak, he just looks at the scared young man in front of him. He's seen a hundred like this one. Men who act tough and talk with bravado, but when the chips are down they all crumble and become sniveling weasels.

"Where is Red staying?"

"They're camped in a small stand of

cottonwoods along that river that runs through town about 15 miles out. What's going to happen to me, mister?"

The kid is clearly scared of being hanged, and that is how Issac wants him, so he ignores the question and asks one of his own.

"How many are with him?"

"He's got 12 men with him besides me and Ben. One of 'em is a big fat man by the name of Big Bob. The others are just drifters who have gathered around Red."

"Bad men seem to find each other in this land." Issac leans forward on his chair. "Were you with him when he sent the woman into town to kill me?"

Lloyd's face pales, and Issac already knows the answer. He can see that the man doesn't want to answer the question, but he waits him out.

"Yes." Lloyd swallows hard. "I overheard him tell her to come ride to town and kill you. He had been manipulating her for a week. I guess you killed her man and she was out of her head. He took advantage of her and convinced her to come to town."

"How did you end up with this outfit, Lloyd? You talk like an educated man."

"I came from money back East, but I came West to make my own fortune. When I heard Ben talking to Red about looking for a gold mine in these parts, I figured it would be my chance to strike it rich, so I rode out with him."

"Don't look for the easy money, son." Issac stands and turns to leave. "I'm gonna let you out of here when I get back, and leave instructions for you to be released if I don't. Let me give you some advice before I go. Go back East and join the family business. You ain't cut out for the West, son."

Without another word, Issac turns and walks away from the cell. He emerges from the jail with a look of determination on his face. Sam Tiller is setting on the porch when he walks out.

"Morning, Sheriff."

"Morning, Sam."

"How are you holding up, Issac?"

"I'm fine, Sam. Just fine. Listen. I've got to do some riding. Do you think we could deputize someone for a couple of days until I get back?"

"Sure, Issac. Who'd you have in mind?" Sam asks, he wants to ask where Issac is going to be riding to, but he doesn't.

"Henry's a solid man. He'll do just fine, unless you've got someone else in mind."

"Sound good to me, Issac."

"There's a man in there that you'll need to let go if I don't come back in a couple of days."

"Sure thing. When you leaving town?"

"Right now."

Issac steps off the porch without another word. He takes off up the street toward his house. Doc Blaine watches him out of his window, and knows by the set of his jaw and the length of his stride that Issac is about to do something he shouldn't be doing in his condition. He runs to the door and yells.

"Issac, where in the hell are you headed?"

"I've got some business to take care of down Santiago way. I shouldn't be gone more than a couple of days."

"What about your arm? You don't need to be riding in the condition you're in."

"I'll be fine, Doc."

Doc Blaine starts to protest, but he can see that Issac isn't going to listen to a word he says, so he just watches him go. In his house, Issac goes about packing his saddlebags with jerky and some bread someone had left on his doorstep as a gift. He fills the loops on his belt with bullets and puts a box in his saddlebags. He puts his other pistol in his belt in front, the butt to his left. He knows he won't be able to use his shotgun any more with one arm, so he leaves it on the rack.

He goes outside and ropes the roan he took from Irons' ranch. Getting the saddle on the horse is much harder than it would have been, but he manages thanks to brute strength. He has to use his mouth to tighten the cinch, but he gets it done. He ties his saddlebags and ground roll behind the saddle, again using his mouth to tie them. Stepping into the saddle, he rides out of Jericho to the south at a fast canter.

He finds a small game trail that runs due south away from town. Turning the roan down the trail, he lets him have his head, as he sits in the saddle and tries to think out how he should go about his task. He goes over what Lloyd told him.

Red and the other are camped 15 miles outside of Jericho in a small stand of cottonwoods along the Snakeskin, the same cottonwoods where Issac killed two members of the Irons' Gang less than a month ago. Besides Red, there is Big Bob, Dan Pullman, and eight others. *Too big of a group to take on all at once. What I need to do is slip in to get a good look at their camp. Maybe I can come up with a plan then.* Lloyd said that Red had sent him and Ben into town to scare him and cause a little trouble.

Riding easy in the saddle, Issac feels good

now that he has something to do. Sitting around and doing nothing just isn't in his nature. Now he has something to take his mind off the death of his daughter. He watches his back trail for dust, just in case Lloyd was lying about him and Ben being the only ones in town. No dust appears on the horizon, but he keeps a watchful eye on the sky anyway.

He slows the roan down to a walk a few miles outside of town, and keeps him at that pace for a while. As he nears the cottonwoods Red is camping in, he skirts to the east a couple of miles. He rides slowly with his hand on his gun butt, ready for action. Once he figures that he is a couple of miles downstream from the outlaws' camp, he finds a group of boulders that provide shade and settles in for the evening. He aims to go in under the cover of darkness and study their camp. He takes the saddle off the roan and lets him roll. Putting the saddle back on the roan, he walks him to the creek for a drink. After picketing his horse in a small patch of grass in the hollow of the boulders, he climbs on top of the biggest one and checks the surrounding country with his field glasses. He can't see anything moving in any direction. Far off to the west, there is a dust trail, but it's miles away and going in the other direction. Climbing down the boulder, he settles into the shade and dozes, trusting the roan to warn him if somebody comes close.

The roan nickering wakes him hours later. He is instantly aware of his surroundings, but he keeps his eyes closed and keeps breathing deeply, as if he's still asleep. Straining his ears for any sound, he hears a boot scrap on gravel off to his left. The sound of a gun being cocked in the same direction lets him know that whoever is out there probably isn't friendly.

"I know you're awake Issac, so stop playing possum."

His mind searches desperately for a face to put to the voice. He keeps still in hopes that the man will think he really is asleep.

"Dammit, Issac, get up!"

Dan Pullman. He recognizes the voice of the former sheriff and member of the Irons' Gang.

Opening his eyes he looks over at Dan, and then right into the barrel of the man's rifle. He eases himself to a sitting position against the rock, careful to keep his hand away from his gun butt. Issac stares at Dan and waits for him to do the talking.

"I thought I saw you ride out of town. I was glassing the town to see what Ben and Lloyd were up to and I heard shooting. Then a while later, I saw you ride out of town in this direction."

"What do you want with me, Dan?"

"Oh, I'm going to kill you, Issac." The fat man gives him a sly smile. "Kill you and take you back to camp, and tell 'em that I gunned you down myself. Won't I be something then? The man that killed Issac O'Connor. The man faster than Randy Houston."

"That won't go over good with Red." Issac says, as he stands to his feet.

"I've already thought that through. I'll wait 'til dark to come into camp, and I'll be holding this here scattergun on him, but in the shadows so he can't see it." Dan pulls out a sawed-off shotgun from behind his back, and shows it to Issac before putting it back. "When he goes for his guns, I'll let him have both barrels, and then I'll be leader of the gang. Think about it: Dan Pullman, leader of the Pullman Gang."

Issac had been waiting for his moment, and when Dan spoke this last line he closes his eyes for a split second longer than normal. Issac takes a step to the right and palms his gun. Dan sees him and tries to bring his rifle to bear, but Issac's gun stabs flame in the coming twilight. He watches Dan sit back hard on his rear end. The fat man's gun goes off, but the shot goes wild. He walks up to Dan, holding his gun on him and kicks the rifle away.

"You always did talk too much, Dan."

He hurries over to his horse and climbs into the saddle, knowing that they would have heard that shot at the camp. He throws his plans to the wind and rides full out for the camp in the cottonwoods. It's completely dark when he enters the camp at a dead run on the roan.

Holding the reins in his teeth, he draws his gun. A man jumps up from his bedroll. Issac snaps a shot and sees the man go down clutching his chest. Charging through the camp at full speed, he snaps a shot at the fire and watches coals fly in every direction. Another man rears up in front of his horse and the roan runs him down. Issac hears him scream as he goes under the churning hooves of the roan.

Big Bob leaps up and Issac snaps a shot at him. The big man turns, as the shot grazes his shoulder. He brings the roan around to the other wise of the camp and charges back through the camp, gun blazing. He empties his pistol, holsters it and draws the other one. He snaps shots left and right at men, as they scramble to find shelter from the flying lead. He hits four of the men for sure and wounds at least two, Big Bob included.

He doesn't want to risk another charge through camp, so Issac whirls the roan and heads for town. The horse is eager to run after the excitement of the camp, so he lets it. A couple of miles from the camp, he slows the horse to a walk and strains his ears for any sign of pursuit. He can't hear anything yet, but he knows that they'll be coming and Red will be fighting mad. *Good. Let him come.* Holding the reins in his teeth once more, Issac breaks open his pistols and thumbs fresh cartridges into them. The process is slow with one hand, but he manages by shoving the barrel of the gun into his waist band.

Knowing that the outlaws will soon be on his trail, Issac turns the roan away from town and heads towards the country, keeping to flat rock and hard packed ground whenever he can to try and lose them, but he knows that Big Bob is the best tracker in these parts, and he isn't sure if he even hit him in his charge through the camp.

He doubles back and rides over his same tracks to confuse anyone that might be trailing him. Riding the roan into the waters of the Snakeskin, he rides for town, crumbling dirt from the bank into the stream every now and then to cover his tracks in the sandy bottom. The sky is a beautiful red from the rising sun when he reaches town. Looking at the red sunrise, he remembers what an Indian chief once told him. 'A red sky in the morning means blood has been spilt this night.'

He rides straight for the livery stable. Inside, he waters and grains the roan, and rubs him down with hay. Walking out, he rounds the livery and holds up his field glasses. Far off in the distance, he can just make out a dust cloud. *Not too big. Probably not more than five men at the most.* He studies the dust cloud for some time, chuckling dryly when it veers to the west and follows his fake trail.

Not wanting anyone else to get involved, he keeps to the shadows of the livery, checking on the outlaw's whereabouts periodically. When the dust trail whirls and starts for town, he knows that they have made his ruse and know where he is. He hurries into the livery and saddles the roan. Leaping into the saddle, he rides hell bent out of town and straight for the oncoming outlaws.

When he reaches a place in the Snakeskin a mile or so out of town, where it cuts through a small rise making a narrow gap in the hill just big enough to hide a rider and horse, he rides in. Settling in, he waits. Time passes slowly, and the heat begins to rise with the sun. Sweat trickles down his neck and chest, as he listens for the riders. He finally hears them.

The roan is a good horse, and Issac has found that he will obey any command given with the legs alone. He waits for the outlaws to ride past the rise, hoping that none of them will decide to ride through the gap looking for an ambush. None of them do. Squeezing the roan with his knees, he rides out of the gap and straight up behind the outlaws.

There are four of them, including Big Bob and Red Houston. Big Bob has a bandage on his right shoulder, but he looks no worse for the wear. Issac lays his hand on his thigh, inches from his gun butt, and raises his voice.

"Hold it right there, boys. Turn around and do it slowly, 'cause I'll plug the first one who makes a move for his gun."

The riders turn their horses slowly around to

face Issac. Red's face burns scarlet when he sees who it is that spoke. He can feel their eyes on the place where his missing arm should be, and can guess that they're wondering if they can beat a cripple to the draw.

"Where's the rest of your gang?"

"They just up and rode away after you attacked out camp." Big Bob explains.

"You should have just rode out with them, Red. I didn't want this, but you pushed the matter. Just like you pushed Jessie into coming to town and killing me." Issac fixes him with a hard stare. "Didn't you?"

"Yeah, I did." Red grins wickedly. "I figured that a woman would be enough to take out your yellow hide."

"You were wrong, Red, and now I'm taking you in."

"I ain't going to jail." One of the other men speaks, his hand inching toward his gun.

"You touch that gun and you'll be dead." Big

Bob tells the man. "Issac here killed Randy Houston, Red's brother."

The man's face pales, and he takes his hand away from his gun, as if it were on fire. Issac can see the hate dancing in Red's eyes at the mention of his bother's name. He knows that the outlaw is about to make his move, and he prays that his old, gnarled hand can grab iron as fast as it used to, just one more time.

"He ambushed him. There's no way this old bastard could get the drop on Randy in a fair fight. He probably shot him in the back."

As Red finishes speaking he draws, his hand is a blur of motion. Issac anticipated this move. Palming his own gun, he fires. Something must have spooked the outlaws' horses, because Issac's first shot takes one of the others in the chest, as his horse leaps in front of Red's. Firing again, he sees his bullet pluck at Red's shirt. Something hits him hard in the ribs and his breath is knocked out of him. Then horses are bucking and jumping all around him. In the fray, he sees Red's horse take out across the country. Red is sawing on the reins and fighting to stay in the saddle.

Issac fires point blank into the face of the other outlaw, as his horse bucks and watches him fall. Big Bob is fighting for control of his own horse, as Issac turns on him and levels his gun. The horse throws the big outlaw from the saddle, and he hits the ground with a thump. He scrambles to his feet and whirls to face Issac. His eyes go wide when he sees the gun pointed at him. He makes like he's going to raise his hands, but his left works its way behind his head. Issac knows that he carries a throwing knife at the nape of his neck and thinks him a fool for going for it, but he doesn't stop him.

Big Bob makes his play for the knife. Issac's gun stabs flame, as the big man drops his knife into the dirt. He looks down at it, confused. Issac's gun roars again and the big outlaw falls. He hits the dirt and tries to rise, but instead he settles back down with a sigh.

Issac thumbs cartridges into his gun, and wheels his horse in the direction in which Red was heading. He rides for a mile before he finds the outlaw. Red is laying on the ground unconscious from hitting his head on a rock by the look of it. His horse is screaming and kicking with a broken leg just beyond him. Issac dismounts and walks carefully over to the fallen man. Taking his guns, he puts them in his waistband and walks over to the horse. He shoots the horse in the head and walks back over to the roan.

Taking a long drink of water, he watches Red, as the outlaw begins to stir around. With a moan, Red sits up and looks at Issac. He gives the outlaw a grin, and tips his canteen in salute. Red's hands drop to his holsters, but he finds them empty. He looks back up at Issac with hate-filled eyes.

"I'm going to kill you." Red shoots a wicked grin at him. "You old son of a bitch."

"I suspect you're going to try."

"You're gonna leave me out here?"

"No." Issac flashes a wicked grin of his own. "I'm going to give you your chance, Red. That's the least I can do. Your brother did the same for me."

"You lie!" Red screams at him. "There wasn't anyone faster than Randy, unless it was me."

"We'll see. Get up, Red."

Red stands to his feet, rubbing his hands. Issac tosses his guns to him one at a time. Red looks down at the guns, and then looks back up at Issac. Smiling, he bends and scoops up the pistol. He places them in his holsters and stares at Issac.

"You just made the worst mistake of you life in giving me back my guns, old man."

"I won't have it said that I didn't give a man a fair chance, Red."

Red lets out a dry chuckle and goes for his guns. His hands blur and his guns stab flame. Issac is faster, but not by much. His own shot crosses Red's only a split second faster. He sees the bullet strike the man in the chest. White-hot fire laces across his cheek, as he lets the hammer fall again. The slug hits Red high on the shoulder and spins him, but he turns right back around, his guns firing. Issac drops to one knee, as a bullet strikes him in the left leg and takes it out from under him. His gun clicks on an empty cylinder, causing him to drop it. Drawing his other gun, he lunges forward at Red and fires as fast as he can slip his thumb off the hammer. Red's body convulses with the impact of the bullets and he goes down, blood turning the front of his shirt crimson.

Issac slumps to his knees, his breath coming in ragged gasps. He stares at the gunman lying dead on the ground before him for a long time, as the sun beats down on his back and the flies circle. The roan finally gets him moving. The horse nudges him in the back with its nose and gives a nicker. Issac reaches up a hand and grasps the stirrup. He pulls himself up slowly with the help of the saddle. His leg tries to buckle as he puts his foot into the stirrup, but he manages to remain standing. He pulls himself into the saddle and slumps forward, blood running freely from the bullet wound in his leg, another in his side and a graze along his cheek bone.

"Take us home, roan."

The horse seems to understand, and starts for Jericho with Issac swaying in the saddle. He stays in the saddle through sheer force of will alone, and somehow he makes it into town. He sees someone rushing up to his horse, which lets him know that he has made it back. Letting go, he slides from the saddle and hits the dirt.

For three weeks, Issac lies in bed, and he is unconscious for two of those weeks. When he finally regains consciousness, he tells his story to the Doc, as well as the rest of the town. Issac wants to get out of bed as soon as he wakes, but the doctor forces him to stay in bed. He tells him that another bout like he just went through will kill him, so Issac complies, and for a whole week he lies around and does nothing. During the week, Deborah brings him his meals. She sits and talks for a long time each time she comes, and Issac realizes that she might just like him. Toward the end of the week, he finds that he just might like her too, and when she comes into his room on the fifth day he asks her.

"Deborah?" Issac sits up on the edge of the bed.

"Yes."

"I ain't got much, but my hands, well, one hand, and a home, but I sure would like it if you would enjoy them with me."

"Was that you asking me to marry you?" She gives him a smile.

"Well, I guess it was." Issac replies angrily. "So what's your answer?"

Deborah shoots him a level stare for a second before she breaks into a smile and wraps him in a hug.

"Of course, Issac." She pulls back from the hug. "Now let's get you something to eat. You're skin and bone."

Issac looks down at what was once a flat stomach, but is now starting to show the signs of a bulge. "Woman, if you keep feeding me like this I won't be able to get in a church to marry you."

"Well get married outside then."

Both of them laugh, as she sets food on the table beside his bed. At the end of the week, Sam Tiller comes in and sits down, a grin on his face.

"How you holding up, Issac?"

"I'm doing fine, Sam. Ready to get out of this bed and start moving."

"Sure you are." Sam chuckles. "You've got Deborah visiting you and bringing you food on a regular basis. Why I bet you ain't even hurt. I bet you've been faking this whole time just to get on her good side."

"The thought never crossed my mind." Issac and Sam share a laugh. "I asked her to marry me, Sam."

"I figured as much. When I went by her shop the other day, she was singing at the top of her lung and sewing a wedding dress. Congratulations."

"Thanks, Sam, but that's not why you came in here, is it?"

Sam's face becomes serious.

"The job of Sheriff is still yours if you want it, Issac."

He dodges the offer with a question. "How's Henry doing at being Sheriff?"

"Good. Good. You were right. He's cut out for the job. There hasn't been a fight in town since he broke up Bob and Jonathan over to the saloon a week ago. But like I said, Issac, the job is still yours if you want it."

"Do you think he could use a deputy that sits around and jaws at the pretty ladies and gets fat in his older years?"

"I think he could." Sam bellows with laughter, his big stomach lurching up and down.

~~~

A week later finds Issac strong enough to leave the doctor's house and move into his own. He mills around for a couple of days, putting off what he knows he hasn't done yet, and doesn't want to do, but he eventually makes himself do it.

Walking up Boot Hill, Issac passes the graves of men he knew and worked with. He passes graves of men he killed and men he saw get killed, young and old alike. The grave he is looking for is almost at the end of the graveyard. He walks up to the rough-hewn cross and drops to his knees. Tracing a finger over the words, 'Abigail O'Connor,' he wonders how he ever ended up here. *How did it get like this?* A tear rolls down his wrinkled cheek, as he stares at the grave of his daughter. Beside it is the grave of his beloved wife.

"I miss you two so very much. I don't know how it ever got like this, but here we are. I hope and pray that you can forgive me for not being able to protect you. I know I can't, but maybe you can. I met a woman who seems to have taken a liking to me. I just thought I would let you know so you wouldn't be mad."

Issac scrubs away his tears and stands up. He looks at the graves of his beloved wife and daughter one last time.

"Goodbye. I love you."

His piece said, he turns and walks away to a different life in the small town of Jericho.

Titles in the series

Made in the USA
Charleston, SC
09 July 2015